A Misunderstanding in Cork City

ORLA KELLY PUBLISHING

Emmett Corbett

LEXICON

A Clinger a type of slow dance where the couple cling to each other barely moving.

A few scoops a few pints, beers.

A lasher a beautiful woman.

Ask for Angela code for distressed women in bars and nightclubs.

Aul-dolls Cork slang for females.

Bad form bad spirited, not a nice thing to do.

Bag of cans cans of beer/ lager.

Balaclava a head covering used for skiing but more commonly skull-duggery.

Bap's *euphemism* for female breasts, from bread baps.

Barry's a popular bar in the upper-middle class area of Cork city

Bazzer a haircut.

Blackrock an affluent area of Cork city.

Bluebottle a big fly commonly found on manure.

Chattie-Boos a term of endearment for female breasts.

Chipper a popular food dipped in batter then deep fried.

Clobber *synonym* for clothing.

Co'mere come here to me, please listen, pay attention to what I have to say.

Cocka-walla an old Corkonian *synonym* for poopoo.

Craic fun, to have a laugh, good time.

Crusty a person with dry crusty bits who doesn't wash themselves.

Derbac M a lotion for nits and crab lice.

Dog very, especially.

Dog-handy very/especially useful.

Dole Social welfare payment.

Dolled-up to be dressed up well, to look good.

Donkey jacket heavy duffel coat lined with plastic shoulders worn by workmen.

Dose of the gallops an expression for diarrhoea. Eg. the Taoiseach got a dose of the gallops at the sight of the protestors. 😁

Douglas an upper-middle class area in the southside of Cork city.

Draws underwear.

Fair-play well done, good for you.

Father Mathew a statue that was reorientated away for the city centre after renovations.

Fean Cork slang for a male.

Fianna Fail dominant political party in Ireland.

Fine Gael dominant political party in Ireland. See Fianna Fail.

Fine-half good looking, an attractive person.

Fivers a five euro note

Gatch a style of walk performed by Gomey's.

Gatt alcohol, drink.

Gentleman Quarters a popular shop for men's clothing in Cork city.

Get the gawk to vomit.

Getting a lip to have a craving for an alcoholic beverage.

Get-up clothes, clothing.

Go'way go away from around me, an expression of disagreement.

Gob mouth.

Gobshite a person who talks shite. (See Taoiseach 😁)

Gomey a buffoon, a person who thinks their fantastic, a dope, someone oblivious to their stupidity.

Grub food.

Guards Irish police.

Hammond lane a scrap yard in Cork city.

Hard-shaw a tough guy. That guard thinks he's the hardshaw.

Having a bang to have a good laugh from something or someone.

Hawking to gaze, stare with hawk eyes.

Hungry article a person greedy for money, see Fianna Fail/ Fine Gael.

I'm sure she's into ya I think she fancies you.

I'm telling ya straight to be forthright and earnest toward someone.

Irelands Own a 100-year-old magazine for rural people.

Jacks toilet.

Jock's underwear.

Lah suffix used to stress importance, look-lah, over there-lah.

Lamp *verb* to look, to direct attention towards. Lamp the state of your-man.

Lined-up to have something ready.

Lumps out of me to take a lot out of someone, to feel overly exerted.

Mangan's clock the traditional place to meet a romantic interest for a date in Cork city.

Manky dirty, unhygienic, unclean.

Manky-yolks an unclean object or person.

Micky-mouse a *synonym* for something small, insignificant.

Monday Club to be in the pub on a Monday instead of work.

MTU Munster Technology University.

Nice-one thanks a lot.

Nobber a person overly excited with romantic intentions.

Paddy a *synonym* for an Irishman oftentimes derogatory depending on the context.

Pepe-le-pew a cancelled cartoon character (see Nobber.)

Play-wide to conduct oneself with vigilance, be alert, to watch out with a wide scope.

Porter a *synonym* for alcohol, booze.

Presentation college an affluent school in Cork city.

Quid money, cash.

Rashers strips of cured bacon popular with Irish breakfast.

Rob Roy a popular bar in Cork city.

Rollie hand rolled cigarette.

RTE Irish State sponsored national broadcaster, known for its extravagant social events, and expensive taste in flip-flops.

Saint Patricks Street the main street in Cork city.

Scoring /Score to get a good result.

Sherbets a posh word for drinks, alcohol.

Shy babies get no jellies a Corkonian *proverb* for, nothing ventured nothing gained.

Slagging to have fun at someone's expense, usually done within the group.

Snack box special a chicken and chips offer held on Tuesdays buy one get one free.

Snooping sneaking, stealing.

South-mall business district of Cork city.

Starkers to be stark naked.

Steamer to be excessively hot under the collar with romantic notions.

Stray-bit a single person.

Sweating bullets to sweat profusely.

Taoiseach Irish head of government, a position periodically held by men of integrity in times past.😁

The corporation city council occasionally known for social housing maintenance and road works etc.

The lord Mayors concert an annual concert held at city hall.

The Northside a working-class area of Cork city.

The state of to observe the condition of a person or thing, always used in a negative in connotation.

There nobody's business a Corkonian idiom for discretion, a plea for privacy, to keep to oneself.

Throwing Bouquets metaphor, to throw bouquets of flowers at one another, to flatter excessively.

Throwing shapes to carry oneself with over confidence, to walk with a swagger (see Gomey)

Todger a *euphemism* for male genitalia.

Tommy-knockers' female breasts.

Tony's Bistro a popular restaurant in Cork city for an Irish breakfast.

Touching cloth an expression for when the poopoo begins to exit without the owner's consent, like a turtles head the cocka began to touch the cloth of the jocks.

Twinkles a posh *euphemism* for nipples.

UCC University College Cork.

West Cork a scenic part of Cork County renowned for its beauty and civil servants.

Western Road an area of Cork city common for student accommodation.

Will-ya will you, used when impatient.

Wind-up to make fun at others expense, to get someone worked-up for fun, (see slagging)

Yolk a thing an object, also used in reference to unsavoury characters.

Your-man He, when speaking of a male person.

Your-wan She, when speaking of a female person.

On the southern coast of a wet and windy isle lies Cork, Ireland's second city. Where business is conducted within a quasi-feudal system, and where the bourgeoisie are beneficiaries of an incestuous lineage of nepotism. Enjoying pensionable jobs within various State and semi-state bodies. It is a city where snobbery, cronyism and class discrimination are hale and hearty, and where its civil servants strive to no longer play second fiddle to Dublin..............

7:00 a.m., Luke's alarm activated.

"What time is it?" asked Máiréad, still half asleep, as she reached for her phone. Realising the time, she yawned "You're an early riser I don't have to be in work till nine."

"Can I make you a coffee?" yelled Luke from across the spacious apartment, while shuffling into his work clothes.

Máiréad stretched with satisfaction within the fine bed linen.

"Last night was wonderful…this bed is wonderful; this whole apartment is huge…I love everything about it… the furniture…the high ceilings…the plush carpet, and the amazing view overlooking the city – how long have you lived here?"

Now fully dressed for work, Luke walked down the kitchen steps with an espresso in each hand. "Live here… oh…I don't live here."

"What do you mean you don't live here?" asked an alarmed Máiréad, swiftly turning to face Luke. "And WHAT are you doing in those dirty overalls?" Her expression quickly shifted to disgust.

Dressed in his painter & decorator overalls, speckled with various colours from previous jobs, Luke nonchalantly replied: "I never told you I lived here."

Now confused and startled, Máiréad recoiled, "But I thought you said last night that you lived here?"

Luke carefully placed the two espressos on coasters on the delicately inlaid side table. "No, I didn't. I said the place was being revamped."

"Is this some kind of dirty trick?" responded Máiréad with increasing agitation.

"A trick?" asked Luke.

"A dirty trick," sneered Máiréad.

Seeing the growing expression of disdain on Máiréad's face, Luke replied "Hang on a minute, you need to calm down and regather your thoughts."

"Regather my thoughts what do you mean 'regather my thoughts'?" screeched Máiréad with murderous looks.

"If you remember…"

"I remember everything!"

Luke coolly reiterated his response, speaking slower than normal in an effort to calm Máiréad. "If you remember, we caught each other's eye from across the bar, and I asked if you would like a drink."

"Yes!"

"We had some cocktails."

"Yes," repeated Máiréad growing irritated.

"We hit it off…had some great conversation, and a great night…what's the matter?"

"But why did you lie about this apartment?"asked Máiréad awkwardly draping a sheet across her chest as she struggled to dress.

Maintaining his composure, Luke answered: "I didn't lie…we finished our cocktails at last call…we went outside…it was raining…and neither of us could flag down a taxi."

"Yes, yes, I remember all that," snapped Máiréad, revealing an ever-increasing country lilt.

Luke, containing his annoyance, continued, "I told you it was a short walk for me and that I was up early in the morning. You asked me where I was going, and I told you to the Metropole apartments. Then you asked me if it would be okay to come with me so that you could phone a cab from here."

"But you told me you were a technician," whined Mairead.

"Yeah, I am… I'm an Artificial Surface Application Technician. It was a joke, and you giggled when I said it."

"But why are you staying here, and where are you really from, are you even from Quork sidiee (CORK CITY)?"

demanded Máiréad as she searched under the sofa cushions for a missing high heel.

Luke, sipping his espresso, almost spat it out. "REALLY from? I never pretended to be from anywhere…where are you REALLY from?"

"Never mind where I'm from…what are you doing in this apartment?"

"I'm working here today."

"What!"

"Yeah, when I couldn't get a cab home to the northside, I didn't see the point of walking home in the rain, so I decided it would be more convenient if I slept here."

Máiréad, now consumed with a sinking feeling, soberly looked at Luke. "You're telling me you're from the northside?"

"Yeah, I am….you say that like it's another planet… why, where are you originally from?"

"NEVER MIND WHERE I'M FROM!" screeched Máiréad. "I feel like such a fool."

Luke, humorously offended, folded his arms, "You feel like a fool. Please enlighten me?"

"Oh, shut up, where's my high heel?"

Luke, determined to inform Máiréad of the facts, responded, "Well, as I recall when we got back here, you asked me if it was okay to stay the night. I made my bed on the couch, offered you the king-sized bed while you initiated a conversation on consent – and cosied up to me."

"Shut up! I remember. I wasn't that drunk."

"You weren't drunk at all," replied Luke, while rummaging through his toolbox and preparing to set up the job.

"Aaaaggghhhaaa!" shrieked Máiréad. "I CAN'T BELIEVE THIS IS HAPPENING TO ME!!"

Luke, now standing at the entrance, opened the front door. "Look, I'm not sure what your problem is. Just a minute ago, you were saying how you had such a wonderful night, and now you're acting erratically, screaming how you feel like such a fool."

Máiréad, refusing to address the events of last night, yelled, "What did you do with my high heel?"

"Now what would I want with one high heel? Look, the lads will be here shortly, and judging by how you're reacting, you might want to leave before they arrive."

"Don't worry, I have no intention of staying," snapped Máiréad, as she reached under the bed to retrieve her stiletto before sitting on an oversized ottoman, strapping up her heel, then clumsily standing to fix herself while texting a friend to collect her.

Just then, the lads – an older painter and two young apprentices – arrived for work.

"Alright, Lukey, what's the craic? Howdya, get on last night?"

"Alright, Francie," said Luke, "I'm surprised to see you here. I thought you'd be in the Monday club today?"

"Shur today's Friday," said Joey, one of the apprentices.

"Yeah, but every day is a Monday club for Francie," laughed Shazer.

"Naah," says Francie. "I must head off later to collect me dole, but I'll be back again after I sign on."

"No hassle," said Luke.

"Alright Shazer, alright Joey, are ye all set for clubbing the weekend?"

"Alright, Lukey," said the apprentices, excited to talk about the club, when suddenly they were disrupted by Francie's coarse, gravelly voice.

"Never mind the club. Who's this lovely lady I see before me…I'm sure I know your face. Do you work in City Hall, or the courthouse or someplace?"

Still smelling of porter from the early-morning house, Francie pulled a comb out of his pocket, slicking back his Brylcreem-drenched strands of hair.

"How are ya love? I'm Francis…have ya any friends?"

Joey burst out laughing, "Go'way, Francie, ya nobber, straight in for the kill. You're old enough to be her grandad."

"And you're old enough to be her sprog, so what's the difference?" replied Francie, slipping the greasy comb back into his pocket. "Anyway, if it's good enough for Hugh Hefner, it's good enough for me."

"Are you seriously putting yourself in the same bracket as Hugh Hefner? Shur, he's a multi-millionaire with a mansion and a magazine," laughed Shazer.

Francie, ignoring the lads, smiled at Máiréad, revealing a palate of brown-to-yellow teeth.

Producing a tattered packet of tobacco, he offered, "Would ya like a rollie?"

Máiréad horrified at Francie's advances and the fact she was recognised, responded in disgust, "I don't smoke," before storming out the door.

Francie turned to Luke. "Co'mere, she's a fine half, where'd ya find her? In fairness, Lukey, you pulls the best of 'em."

"Yeah, if I do, you scare them off with the steam evaporating from under your collar... look, she even ran off without her phone."

Máiréad, now in the lobby, saw her friend outside then rushed out to meet her. "Oh, thanks for coming Fionnuala. Let's get out of here I could badly do with a frappé."

"Well, how did you get on last night?" asked Fionnuala in a brash west Cork twang.

As she was just about to answer Máiréad was interrupted by a homeless man, "Excuse me Miss, any chance you could spare some change for a cuppa tea?" "Oh, piss off, I'm sick of dealing with you dregs." Scowled Máiréad.

Then clutching her purse, she realised, "Wait, where's my phone…oh nooo, I rushed out the door without it,"

"No probs, I'll wait here while you go up and get it, " said Fionnuala as she went to sit on the lobby chair.

"No…I can't; there's a dirty old man up there, and I don't want to go back up on my own…I need you to accompany me."

"Wait…what were you doing in Metropole apartments with a dirty old man?"

"Please don't ask…it's a long story, and I'm too traumatised to even think about it."

"Are you ok? Will I call the Guards?"

"No, I'm grand…no need for the Guards. I'm just an idiot for getting my wires crossed."

Máiréad, admiring Fionnuala's style, suddenly notices that her snug top is revealing in more ways than one.

"Fionnuala, where's your bra?"

"Oh…I've decided not to wear one."

"Why not?"

"Because it's much more progressive and liberating to go braless. Anyway, I don't see why I should conform to the constraints of a chauvinistic, patriarchal society."

"But your twinkles are showing!"

Fionnuala, a buxom country lass, full of notions but of good farming stock, defiantly declares: "I don't care; it's my body, and if I don't want to wear a bra, then I don't see why I should!"

"But Fionnuala…your twinkle stars are on display for everyone to see…you'll attract unwanted attention."

"Look, Máiréad, we shouldn't have to worry about Objectifying Pigs. If somebody wants to be a sordid troglodyte, that's their problem."

"But we definitely can't go up there now!" replied Máiréad with a whinge.

"Why not?"

"There are construction workers up there!"

"Oh, nonsense," says Fionnuala, "I have plenty of experience with construction workers. My brother Cormac is studying engineering at UCC, and my cousin Oisín is an architect."

Máiréad, stone-faced, looks her dead in the eye.

"But Fionnuala, these people are painters." Fionnuala gulps, "As in plural?"

"Yess four of them," replied Máiréad.

"But I thought you said there was just a dirty old man?"

"Look, no time to explain. We'll be in and out really quickly...now let's just get my phone before it gets stolen."

"Ok," said Fionnuala with a less brazen demeanour.

Back in the apartment, the lads were preparing the workspace.

"Francie, make sure to cover the furniture with the dust sheets before you paint that ceiling," shouted Luke.

"I'm doing it," says Francie, pulling the dust sheet out over the king-sized bed.

"What's this?" asked Francie, discovering an elaborate knicker at the end of the bedpost.

Glancing over both shoulders, with his sly, beady eyes, Francie stealthily stuffed the panties into his pocket. "I'll take care of them," utters he with a smirk.

"What are you doing shoving a knickers into your pocket Francie?" asks Shazer.

"What knickers?"

"The one you crammed into your 1980s Levi's", replied Shazer. "If Luke saw that he'd snap."

"Yeah," says Joey. "How would you like someone snooping around your smelly Y-fronts?"

"Oh, yaauck," groan the two apprentices, now gagging at the thought of Francie's undies.

"Sure, who'd want those crusty old jocks anyway… it'd be like Mr. Hankey was joyriding in them, with all the skid marks," laughs Shazer.

"I know, yeah," said Joey. "They might want them for their Petri dishes at the College, shur they'd probably find a cure for AIDS."

"Whaaahhhhaaah ha ha!"

"Or North Korea might want them for use in a biological weapon."

The two apprentices buzzed off each other as they wound Francie up.

"I'm going to give it back to her when I see her," croaked Francie with dubious sincerity.

"You will, yeah!" mocked the two boys.

"Of course, I will," says Francie in an attempt to save face.

Startled, Francie jumped to the sound of three loud thumps on the apartment door.

Luke opened the door, confronted by Máiréad and Fionnuala. "I'm getting my phone," demanded Máiréad as she pushed past Luke. "Where is it?"

"I just had it there two minutes ago. I left it on the side table for you."

"Out of my way," demanded Máiréad, hastily looking under the dust sheets, undoing the lad's work.

"I'll ring it there from my phone," offered Luke.

"I don't think so…delete my number from your phone. Fionnuala will do it."

Luke shouted across the apartment to the apprentices, "Boys, look around for that phone so we can get back to work."

Noticing the young lads chuckling away to themselves, Luke couldn't help but overhear the apprentices, "Wait till Francie sees them."

Now gawking at Fionnuala, Francie imprinted her every feature with piercing appreciation.

With a breath-wafting forth, evocative of the tooth fairy taking a shite in a rotten cavity, Francie melodically panted into Máiréad's face:

"Haaalloo again, and I see you brought a friend."

Almost gagging with repulsion, the girls leaned back as if to do the limbo.

Gasping, with a cricked neck, Máiréad recoiled in repulsion.

"We're just getting my phone, and we'll be gone again."

"I thought she might be the friend I was asking ya about," winked Francie.

"Francie, leave the girls alone and help the boys look for her phone," said Luke.

Francie clasped his hands with enthusiasm, then beckoned the apprentices.

"For feck's sake…did ye see the tommyknockers on your-wan?"

"I know yeah," said Joey with excitement. "It must be freezing out."

Joey now staring at Fionnuala, says out the side of his mouth: "Shur, they're nobody's business…you'd hang a wet donkey jacket off them!"

"Well, you're definitely making them your business, the way ye keep hawking at her," said Shazer. "Come on will ye…help me find the phone."

"Feck it," said Francie "They'd smoother ya…the last time I saw a pair of baps like that was down the dance hall."

"Are you on about my Nan again?" snapped Joey in a touchy tone.

"Ahh…shur that was ages ago…and to give credit where credit's due, Kathleen always had a fine heaving bosom… fair play to her."

"Leave my Nan's name out of it, ya steamer," replied Joey.

"Back in the good aul' days, Francie, was it?" asked Shazer, bouncing the two lads off each other for a rise. "Sure, the wimmin used be all over me back then, " his voice full of reminiscence.

"They used, yeah Francie," laughed the lads with amusement.

"They uussed…shur when I was ye're age, me arse used be going like a fiddler's elbow. Ask your Nan, she'd tell ya all about it."

"I'm telling you now, Francie, that's my Nan you're talking about," snapped Joey.

"Ahhh...noo... not like that at all...I'm on about jiving... we used be out jiving on the dance floor, shur it's all in the hips...the mashed potato, an' all that."

"You smell like mashed potatoes, ya mank," said Joey.

"I'd say he was like a rat on top of a dirty spud," laughed Shazer.

"Shut up you, stirring things as usual," said Joey with a cranky stare.

RING...RING...RING...RING.

"I can hear it ringing," said Fionnuala, scratching nervously at the sight of Francie's beetle-juice grin.

"It's coming from over by you," said Luke to the lads.

"Ring it again," squawked Francie, now winking at Fionnuala. "I think I hear it."

Luke, frustrated at the delay, whispered to Joey:

"Will you stop ogling her friend, and close your mouth."

"I can't help it, Lukey," said Joey, "I'm distracted... they're like two bottles of Budweiser."

"And I'm getting a lip for a gatt," laughed Francie.

Shazer burst out laughing, shouting "bottles of Budweiser!" as he bent over in stitches.

"Joey's got a point," said Francie, "She's like Dolly Parton."

"Dolly Parton on steroids," said Joey.

Shazer laughed even harder. "Dolly Parton, aaahhhhaaa ha ha, she's about 90!"

"Well, Pamela Henderson so."

"Pamela who?"

"Henderson," replied Francie.

"Aaahhhhhgghhhaaaaaa…. it's Pamela Anderson… when was the last time you watched telly?" laughed Shazer.

"Shur, what do I want a telly for…the ads were on this morning down the pub and all that was on it was maxi-pads and hairy armpits…I nearly got the gawk into me pint…anyway, who's the famous wan now, for the chattie-boos?"

"Chattie-boos…. for feck's sake, Francie…stop will ya. I can't breathe, and me ribs are hurting me," said Shazer. And the two apprentices howled with laughter.

"I found it," says Luke, handing the phone over to Máiréad.

"Lads, cover the furniture again," yelled Luke.

Full of mischief, Shazer pulled Francie aside to give a coaxing word of encouragement.

"Here, Francie, I think you should ask her out…I'm sure she's into ya."

"Do ya really think so?" asked Francie. "Cause she keeps looking away and scratching every time she sees me."

"Don't mind that boy…she's just playing coy," said Shazer.

"Maybe she has the itchy and scratchies," murmured Francie. "Anyway, if she does, I've a half a bottle of Derbac M at home."

Throwing shapes like 'The Fonz' from 'Happy Days', Francie adjusted and fine-tuned with the greasy comb, oblivious to Shazer's sniggers.

"Lamp the gatch on him" whispered Joey, "I'm sure he thinks he's John Travolta."

Still gawping at Fionnuala from across the room, Francie strutted over with delusional self-assurance, imparting his proverbial wisdom.

"Shur, shy babies, get no jellies."

As the girls are just about to leave, Francie approached.

"Here, Fionnuala, gis your number there, and we'll get a snack box special some Tuesday."

Pulling his Mars bar-sized Nokia out of his pocket, Máiréad's knickers fell on the floor.

"For feck's sake," blurted Francie.

Máiréad, appalled, gasped: "What are you doing with my underwear?"

"Oh...ehh...I just found your draw's over there when looking for your phone...I just wanted to give them back to ya."

"Oh, my gosh, Máiréad!" exclaimed Fionnuala. "You didn't?"

"OF COURSE, I FREAKING DIDN'T! I told you it's a long story," screamed Máiréad, as she seized her panties back with a snatch from Francie, who halfheartedly attempted to pick them back up off the floor.

Máiréad, sunk with mortification, stuck her head into Francie's face.

"How very subtle of you, your prudence knows no bounds...come on, Fionnuala, let's get out of here," before slamming the door.

"Feck it...what was her problem?" said Francie to the lads who were now doubled up in hysterics.

"Alright boys, back to work. This apartment won't paint itself," said Luke, now happy to see the end of all the dramatics.

Consumed with a disorientating blend of fury and humiliation, Máiréad made a beeline for the receptionist in the apartment lobby.

"I would like to speak to the manager please."

"One moment," replied the lady at the desk.

Shortly after, a tall, smartly dressed, elegant woman with a well-spoken manner invited Máiréad into her office.

"Good morning, I'm the manager, how can I help you?"

"Yes" said Máiréad, "I would like to make a complaint."

"I'm sorry to hear that. What would be the prob….?"

Máiréad hastily interjected. "Somebody is using an apartment without the owner's knowledge."

"Oh, really! Please tell me which apartment that is, and I'll contact security immediately."

Máiréad, now out for blood, quickly conveyed: "It's the penthouse apartment."

"I'm afraid that's not possible," replied the manager. "Why not?"

"The homeowner is actually occupying that apartment as we speak."

"But there is a painter & decorator using the resident's apartment without their knowledge his name is Luke," blurted Máiréad.

"Oh, that would be Mr Davis," she said with a smile. "Who?"

"Luke Davis, he's up there right now in his painting overalls."

"Yes, that's him."

"I'm afraid you must be mistaken."

"No, I'm not" avows Máiréad, now frustrated from the morning's events.

"Well, if it's the penthouse apartment, then I'm afraid you are."

"How can I be?"

"Mr Davis is the homeowner; and he's having his place redecorated at the moment."

Máiréad, resolute, queried the manager. "But he told me he doesn't live there, and what's he doing in those shabby painting overalls?"

"Well, he doesn't live there, and Mr Davis is well known as a hands-on worker."

"But who lives there so?"

Mr Davis has several properties throughout the city, which he operates as Airbnbs."

"What!"

"Yes. Mr Davis is a valued tenant and has quite the portfolio."

"What!" screeched Máiréad. "How so?"

"Well, it's common knowledge that, just before the 2008 financial crisis, Mr Davis sold his painting company in New York, eventually returning home to make some shrewd property investments."

"New York...investments?" repeats Máiréad, shocked at the emerging facts.

The manager, guiding Máiréad to a wall full of photos, responded: "Look, there's his picture at the Lord Mayor's Concert."

Máiréad gazed at the alcove of framed photographs, only to see Luke, dressed in a tuxedo, mingling with other business people whom she recognised from City Hall.

"How didn't I know this?" mumbled Máiréad under her breath.

As a gob-smacked Máiréad stared at the wall, the manager continued: "The lads helping him are his nephews and, of course, there's Francis, who is an old neighbour of mine from Blackrock."

Thinking she couldn't be more shocked, Máiréad responded, "Wait Francis is from Blackrock?"

"Oh, yes," replied the manager. "He used to play rugby with my brother for Cork Con. In fact, he was also captain of the school team for Presentation College."

Then, tipping off in a soft voice, the manager divulged: "And although he was the black sheep of his family, he was quite the athlete back in his day."

"But what about Luke…I mean Mr Davis…where does he live?"

"Respectfully, that's his own business," replied the manager. "But I believe he also has several properties on the northside and adjacent outskirts."

"Nooooo!" cried Máiréad with a moan, now feeling sick to her stomach.

"Are you ok?" asked the manager. "You look kind of pale, maybe you should sit down."

"No, thank you," whimpered Máiréad in a timid, trembling voice. "I must go now."

Máiréad turned to walk toward the brass-polished revolving entrance which felt miles away.

Exhausted, she edged closer with baby steps at a snail's pace.

Unexpectedly, the manager taps her on the shoulder.

"Excuse me, Miss."

"Huh," says Máiréad, with a drained, facial expression.

"I think you dropped something."

"What is it?" asked Máiréad.

The manager pointed to the lobby floor, while Máiréad simultaneously turned to bend in the same direction.

In a trance-like state, Máiréad picked up the dropped item, finally realising what she held in her hand – was her nimbly pleated panties.

Meanwhile back in the apartment, Luke said to the lads, "Right boys I'm off, I must go meet some clients." "No hassle Luke, we'll finish up here," said Shazer.

"Feck it, them wimmin can be contrary out," said Francie.

"Contrary out," said Shazer. "You had her *Anne Summers* stashed in your pocket, it's no wonder she was contrary."

"Ahh shur that was ages ago," said Francie, "I'm starving let's get some grub, we deserve a break after all that."

"They do nice rolls in that coffee shop on McCurtain Street," said Joey.

"I'll follow ye over," said Francie "I must collect me dole first."

****

The lads were sitting in the coffee shop eating their lunch, when they noticed Francie being served in the café, then walking toward them smiling like Freddie Kruger.

"What's he grinning at?" asked Shazer.

Francie sat down next to the lads and finished his coffee in three sups, then immediately got up to get another.

Shazer turned to Joey "Is he feeling alright drinking those coffees at €3.90 a pop?"

"I know yeah," said Joey. "That's out of character for him, shur he's so mean, he turns off the gas when turning the rashers."

Shazer laughed "Ha-ha, shur they call him 'follow the coffin down the pub', he's goes to everyone's funeral for the free sandwiches and the piss up."

Joey burst out laughing "I heard he bought a load of broken chocolate for Easter, and said he fell coming up the steps."

Shazer laughing even more replied, "Shur he told his niece on her communion day, that his gas metre was her savings box."

"Whhhaaaahhhaaa," laughed the two boys.

"Shush, play wide, here he comes again with a big smile on his face," said Joey.

"What are ye laughing at?" asked Francie.

"Never mind what we're laughing at, what are you grinning at when you just spent €7.80 on two mickymouse coffees?"

"I'm sure your-wan fancies me," said Francie.

"Who?" asked Shazer. "That fit looking lasher on the till?"

"Shur she's way out of your league," said Joey "Anyway I'm sure your-man in the muscle top is her fella."

"Goway will-ya, I was scoring with lashers when you were being washed in the sink, and aul Chippendale better keep away, or hell get a gluten free clatter into the face."

Joey winked at Shazer, "Shur he'd mangle you, look at the size of him."

"He would yeah," said Francie "they'll have to call the corporation to dig me out of him."

"What makes you think she's into ya?" asked Shazer.

"Shur look at me cup," said Francie.

"What about it?" asked the lads.

"Look-lah, didn't she make a love heart on the top of it for me," smiled Francie.

The boys burst out laughing and doubled over.

"What are ye laughing at ye dopes, shur she done it twice for me," snarled Francie.

"They do that with every coffee ya mad thing," laughed the lads.

"They do yeah," said Francie.

Joey began to mimic Francie "Shur she done it twice for me…you're like UK Gold with all the repeats."

"And you'll be full of breaks like RTE if you keep it up." Said Francie with a saucy stare.

"I'll prove it to ya," said Shazer. "We all get coffees for the road, and see if she puts a love heart on all of them."

"Anyway," says Shazer, "I thought you were doing online dating?"

"I was, shur Joey set it up for me. I had one date and got banned."

Joey laughed. "Shur he gave me a photo for his profile picture, in his 20s wearing a rugby jersey."

Shazer laughed. "Catfishing were we, Francie? What did ya get banned for?"

"I've no idea," answered Francie. "I met your-wan in a disco bar in town, but the moment I asked her what she wanted to drink, she ignored me and kept asking the barman for Angela. I'd say she was a lezzy!"

"So, your gone off the app so Francie?" asked Shazer.

"I am, but I've gone back to the old reliable," said Francie pulling an issue of Irelands Own out of his jacket. "I've an aul stray-bit lined up an all for tonight."

"Is that the country woman you were texting?" asked Joey. "Here Shazer, you should see the text messages he sent her…. I can't wait to take you out for a clinger, my darling."

Shazer laughed, "Francie got game so, is it?"

"He sure does," smiled Joey.

"Is she good looking Francie?" asked Shazer.

"Well, I'm actually breaking me cardinal rule by going on a blind-date," replied Francie.

"What's your cardinal rule?" asked Joey.

"Finding a wife is like buying a Jack Russel, you need to see the mother and father first." The boys laughed.

As they were having the banter, the young lady on the till began clearing the tables.

With that Francie drops a spoon on the floor, and Joey leaned over to pick it up.

"Leave it there ya dope, she's coming over now," said Francie.

"Did you just drop that spoon on the floor, just so you could check out your-wans arse?" asked Shazer.

Joey bursts out laughing, "You're some nobber Francie, I'm telling ya straight,"

"What are ye on about," said Francie "Let the girl do her job, shur haven't we done enough work this morning."

"Well break time is over," said Shazer "we need to take the gear out of the apartment."

As the lads get up to leave, Francie smiled at the girl on the till and said with a wink "Bonjour senorita, one more coffee for the road love."

The girl made Francie's coffee and put a heart on top, then served Shazer and Joey, doing the same.

Francie's grin swiftly withered, as the lads walked outside the door.

"She's some hussy, I'm telling ya straight, €11.70 for three coffees. All she's short is a balaclava with prices like that," said a sulky Francie.

Shazer then whispered to Joey, "The last time I seen him this angry was when we filled an empty football full of rocks and asked him to play penalty shootout."

The boys burst out laughing.

"Come on, let's go up to the apartment and take away the gear," said Joey.

After arriving, they noticed the radio was left on.

"Ye left me radio on, wasting all me batteries," said a cranky Francie. "And who turned on Corky FM, I can't stand them."

The local talk show had just started. "It's the Sonny Prendergast Show, and here's your host Sonny."

Francie shouted over "Turn off those self-indulgent gobshites off, for feck's sake all they be doing in banging on about Cork and how great Cork is…throwing bouquets at each other."

"Shur we only listen to it for the slagging," said Shazer.

"Their either bragging or moaning, and misery loves company," said Francie.

"Turn it up there, and we'll have a bang off them," laughed Joey.

The lads turned up the conversation on the radio.

Sonny: "Just to remind you guys, that were having a competition for a €500 voucher for Gentleman Quarters, for whoever can say the most flattering things about Cork."

"See I told ya" said Francie "out fishing for compliments as usual."

Sonny: "Next on the line we have Claire, what's on your mind Claire?"

Claire: "Hi Sonny, I just wanted to say, that I was having my dinner yesterday, and that a bluebottle landed on my plate, but I left him there to eat away because I think it's good for nature and the environment to have its fill."

Sonny: "WOW, what a very magnanimous thing for you to do, you know I'm always blown away by the generosity of Cork people, even letting the insects eat away at their food before they do."

Claire: "Well Sonny I think we should all care about the ozone layer."

Sonny: "Amazing."

Suddenly Francie shouted out from across the room, "Cockaaaa!"

The boys turned around to see what Francie is shouting about.

"What's up Francie?" asked Joey. "Cockaa….Cockaa-Wallaaa…" shouted Francie as he hurried toward the toilet like John Wayne on fast forward.

Pushing Shazer out of the way Francie yelled, "TOUCHING CLOTH!"

Joey turned to Shazer, "I'd say he has a dose of the gallops, after all those coffees."

While Francie was in the toilet sweating bullets, Shazer pulled Joey aside "Here we should enter that competition on the radio, and if we win, we can get Francie a makeover. He be all set for his date tonight."

"He will need more than fresh set of clobber to doll him up, we'd have to hit him with the pressure washer… shur I heard he got bitten by a rat, and the rat had to get a tetanus," laughed Joey "and one of the boys said they saw him in the toilet in McDonalds washing his feet in the sink."

"He'll be grand, there's a steam room down in the hotel, we could stick him in there for an hour," smiled Shazer.

"I'll ring the show and you'll go on the phone," said Shazer.

"Why do I have to go on the phone?" asked Joey.

"Because you're good at doing accents."

"What's that got to do with anything?"

"Because Sonny loves people from other counties saying how much they love Cork; it will increase our of chances of winning."

Shazer handed Joey the phone. "Here it's ringing." "What do I do?" asked Joey.

"Just pretend you're from up the country somewhere." "Where?"

"Tipperary or Waterford. Use your imagination."
"How do I do their accent?" asked Joey.

"Just talk like a Traveller," said Shazer.

Joey got on to Corky FM.

Sonny: "Welcome to the Sonny Prendergast show, who do we have on the line?"

Joey answered "Hoy Sonny, its Pa here, I originally from Tipperary, but I've been living in Cork for the past ten years, and I just want to say it's the best thing I ever done and how much I love the Cork and the Cork people."

Sonny: "WOW that's great. How so? What is it about us Cork people you find so amazing?"

Joey looked at Shazer in need of a prompt "Just keep saying the word Cork," whispered Shazer.

"Well Sonny, the Cork people are so brilliant and Cork people are so generous, and clever, and I think ye have the best radio station in Cork," replied Joey.

Sonny: "WOW that's great, tell me more."

"And I think the other 31 counties in Ireland have so much to learn from Cork and the Cork people living in Cork," added Joey, really getting into his stride now. Sonny rings a bell in his studio, DING DING DING.

Sonny: "Well, I think we have a winner for our €500 voucher for Gentleman Quarters hooray for you Pa."

"Hoy, thanks a bunch Sonny, you're a star, and keep taking them aul politicians to task, exposing the pettiness," says Joey.

"Aaahagggaha! ZIP UP YOUR PANTS."

Joey and Shazer jump around to see where the scream came from, and see a middle-aged couple standing right behind them, with the lady pointing over their shoulders.

Looking at where she is pointing, they see Francie after exiting the toilet.

"Francie, your todgers' hanging out," yell the lads.

"Oh, for feck's sake," says Francie "I forgot to tuck him in. Those coffees took lumps out of me. I'm all wrong after them. Sorry about that," said Francie unfazed.

Turning back to the couple, Shazer asked "How can we help ye? Are ye lost?"

The man replied, "We're thinking of leasing this apartment from Luke, and we just wanted to look around before we make our decision."

"Well look away," said Francie as he zipped up his fly, "We were just leaving."

As Francie walked past the couple with a bundle of dust sheets folded in his arms, he whispered into the man's ear with a wink.."The dramas nobody's business, I had me fair share of it meself this morning."

The man stood there bewildered as Francie headed off down the stairs to load up the van.

"What is that smell? It's putrid," asked the lady covering her nose with a handkerchief.

"Oh, that would be Gonk," said Joey.

"What's Gonk?"

"It's like a mix of piss and toe-jam combined," said Shazer.

"Please tell me that was coming from his feet," said the lady.

"Well, that up for debate." says Shazer.

"But it's definitely coming from below his waist, we know that much," said Joey.

"How long will it linger for?" asked the lady.

"Give it about 40 minutes," answered Shazer.

"Which is a lot less I can say about the visual; that image will be burned into our psyches forever," said Joey as he shook his head with a tut.

"Right, we're off, enjoy your look-around. Pull the door out when you're done." says Shazer.

After loading up the van, Joey called Francie over. "Here Francie come with us across town, we have a surprise for you."

As the lads walked over the bridge, and down Saint Patrick's Street, Francie said, "This town has gone to the dogs, even Father Mathew has turned his back on it."

Just then, the lads are obstructed by a pudgy looking individual sticking a clipboard in their faces. With a thick pair of glasses that somehow enhanced his gullible stare, he addressed Francie in a mild Dublin accent.

"We're protesting here today and would like you to sign our petition."

Francie answered "Maybe some other time bud, we're kind of busy today."

The protester indignantly responded "Typical, we're trying to end 400 years of oppression, and indifferent people like you are part of the problem," waving a leaflet aggressively in Francie's face.

"Shur we have enough troubles to worry about. Look around, the city is starving, why don't ya do something closer to home?" replied Francie.

"Four hundred years of oppression man, four hundred years," repeated the protester, now invading Francie's personal space.

Francie stared back at the protester, "I'll see your 400 years, and I'll raise ya 800, now feck off out of my way before I break the windows in around your face, and it won't take me 400 years to do it either."

The protester gulped, and scampered off with his tail between his legs.

"What did I tell ye lads, gobshites everywhere…now where are we off to?" asked Francie.

The lads stopped outside Gentleman's Quarters. "Come on in Francie, were getting you a new rig-out," said Shazer.

"Shur hold on to your money boys, I'm grand," said Francie.

"It's alright, we won the prize on the radio, well look after ya," said Joey.

"Are ye sure? Cause your-man in there is some salesman. You go in for a jock's and come out wearing three-piece suit."

"It's grand boy, we've got a €500 voucher," said Shazer.

"That's the job boys, nice one, I always tell Luke, yere great young-fellas."

As Francie was getting fitted for his clothes, the two lads began slagging him.

"And here comes Francie in a nice snazzy number… give us a twirl there Francie, you're like a fella from off the runway," joked Joey.

Francie laughed, "Lucky you have that €500 voucher, or I'd be doing a run-away," making the lads laugh.

After paying for the clothes, Shazer said "Right two more things to do."

"What's that Shazer?" asked Francie.

"My sisters a dental hygienist, and said she can fit you in on her break, then we go back to the hotel for a steam-room, and we'll be ready to paint the town red," said Shazer.

"Or paint the town brown Francie, if you have any more of those coffees," smirked Joey.

Shazer laughed, "You'll be like a shiny new penny for your date tonight."

"Let's go so," said Francie "Shy babies get no jellys."

After leaving the steam-room, the lads are all dolled-up ready for a night on the town.

Fixing himself in the mirror Joey said to Shazer, "That voucher was dog handy. We were able to get some new get-up for ourselves an-all out of it."

"I know yeah," said Shazer. "Where's Francie? Is he ready yet?"

Just then Francie stepped out of the dressing room, with his dirty old clothes in the new shopping bags.

The lads started whistling, "Look at you Francie, you're like a fella from down the South Mall," said Shazer, "And

Joey was saying, we should get ya an underpants made of fivers, just in case you don't score tonight, but I think you'll be grand all spruced up like Logan Roy."

"I know yeah," said Joey, "fair play to ya Francie, you scrub up well."

Francie grinned at himself in the mirror checking out his cleaned teeth, that had just been descaled.

"Shazer, fair play to your sister for fitting me in, the wimmin won't know what hit them when they see these dazzlers."

"No probs," said Shazer. "She said your choppers were a bit stubborn at the start, but as soon as she used the Calgon for cleaning the washing machine, the plaque came right off."

Francie smiled. "I'm going leaving Finbarr in the van to mind the gear, he'll keep an eye on it for us, just in case somebody tries to breaks in."

Finbarr was Francie's Jack Russel that he took everywhere with him. A vicious little bastard with a hunting pedigree for badgering.

"I pity the fella who tries to go near the van with Finbarr inside, he'll get ripped apart…shur he's better than any car alarm," said Joey.

"Right boys I'm off now," said Francie, "I can't be keeping the damsels waiting. Nice one for looking out for me."

"No probs Francie, have a great night bud."

"You too lads, and keep out of trouble, whatever ye do."

Francie walked over to Saint Patrick Street to meet his date under Mangan's clock, when he is approached by an attractive voluptuous woman.

"Hello there, I'm Breeda. Are you Francis?"

Francie stunned at her beauty just stared at her gobsmacked, then answered with a stutter, "I am. I'm Francis please to meet you Breeda."

"I don't get up to the city much," said Breeda, "So where's a good place to go?"

"I know a grand place not far from here. Do you like steak?" asked Francie.

Breeda smiled, "You're talking to a beef farmers daughter. Lead the way."

Francie brought Breeda to Issacs restaurant and got seated at a table for two before the waiter approached. "Can I take your order?"

"I'll have a pint of Murphy's," said Francie. "What would you like Breeda?"

"I'll have the same."

Francie looked at Breeda as if he just hit the jackpot.

"Are you ready to order food?" asked the waiter.

"I'll have the steak," says Francie.

"How would you like it done?"

"Cut off his horns and give his ass a good wipe," joked Francie, thinking he's hilarious.

"I'll have the same," laughed Breeda. "You know Francis, I find the older I get, the rarer I like it."

Francie stared into Breeda's eyes from across the table. "I know exactly what you mean Breeda, I know exactly what you mean."

After finishing the meal Francie asked, "How do you feel about a bit of dancing Breeda?"

Breeda smiled. "Sure, why not, I haven't been dancing in years."

"Sounds like a plan," said Francie. "There's a great craic over in the Rob Roy."

"Lead the way Francis," smiled Breeda.

Over in the Rob Roy, Francie ordered the drinks, then took Breeda out for a jive on the floor. After a few songs, Breeda said to Francie, "I'm having such a great night Francis, I didn't have this much fun in years."

"How long have you've been single?" asked Francie.

"My husband passed away seven years ago, our kids are grown and I just felt life is too short, and he would want me to be happy."

"I'm sorry to hear that," said Francie. "How many kids do you have?"

"I have a son and a daughter, but they live in the city."

"Well, I hope I'm good company for you tonight," replied Francie.

Breeda laughed "You are of course Francis, but my daughter would have to vet you all the same, she's very protective of me. She calls down every weekend for a cuppa tea and a chat."

"Well, if she's anything like you Breeda, I'm sure we'd get along just fine," smiled Francie. "Now if you excuse me Breeda I must just go to the Gents."

While relieving himself at the urinal, a stranger says to Francie with a chuckle, "I see you jiving away out on the floor having a ball, I might head out myself later for a dance. You could have some competition on your hands."

Francie turned to the stranger with a vicious stare. "Competition…what do you mean competition?"

The stranger now rattled realised he made a mistake

striking up conversation with Francie. "Ah sure I'm only joking; all I'm saying is for men our age you've fierce energy."

"You didn't see the half of it yet," snarled Francie.

"Look I don't want any trouble, all I'm saying is you're a good dancer, I wish I could dance like that, only for I have a bad leg."

Francie stuck his head into the stranger's face and ground his teeth. "A bad leg, tell me what's wrong with your leg?"

The stranger gulped, "Old age."

"I don't know about that," said Francie, "The other leg is the same age and there's nothing wrong with it, you seem well able to me."

Just then someone enters the toilet, and the stranger runs out the door. As Francie looks out to see where he went, he sees Breeda waving over.

Francie smiled back then sat down to order some more drinks.

Breeda smiled at Francie. "Francis cancel the drinks, my neighbour is throwing a shindig at her house, would you like to go?"

"Shur the night is still young," said Francie with a grin. "Lead the way."

As Francie and Breeda got into the mini bus, he saw Shazer and Joey walking up Oliver Plunket Street. Francie tapped the window to call the lads. They looked around to see who was calling them, but the street was so crowded they didn't see Francie.

"I'm sure I heard someone call our names," said Joey.

"Me too," said Shazer.

"There's a bar at the top of the street with a big queue. It must be a good aul spot. Will we give it a go?" said Joey.

"Let's go," said Shazer.

The lads stood in a multicultural queue with people for about 20 minutes.

"Co'mere this queue is like the United Nations," said Joey.

When they finally reached the top of the queue, a skinny looking bouncer with a scraggy goatee puts out his hand.

"ID?" asked the bouncer.

The lad's handed over their IDs, "Here you go."

"Where were ye tonight?" asked the bouncer.

"Nowhere, we just finished work," answered Joey.

"Not tonight, I think ye have too drink on board," said the bouncer.

"We didn't even have a drink," said Shazer.

"Not tonight I said, now move away from the door."

"What do ya mean move away from the door, you just left in everyone before us and we're sober?" replied Shazer.

Without even looking at the lads the bouncer said, "Management has the right to refuse admission. Move away from the door."

Joey pulled Shazer by the arm, "Come on Shazer, let's try somewhere else."

Shazer infuriated walked away. "Try somewhere else, that's the fourth bar we've been refused out of and were not even drunk."

"I know yeah," said Joey.

"That skinny piss-ant thinks he's the hard-shaw, I'd drag him out through the sleeve of his shirt. The only reason he refused us was because of our accent," said Shazer in a temper.

As the lads were walking down the street, they passed some homeless people who were begging.

"Feck this," said Shazer as he approached the homeless lads. "Here boys, I'll give ye €20 for the hats."

The homeless lads gladly handed over their tattered hats and take the money.

"What do you want with two manky hats?" asked Joey.

"Here," said Shazer, "You take the wine one and I'll take the mustard one."

"I'm not wearing that yolk, I'll get nits," said Joey.

"Just try it on," said Shazer, "and roll it up all the way to your forehead."

Joey rolled up the beanie hat. "Now what?"

"Ok," said Shazer, "Now roll up your jeans to your ankles and button your shirt all the way to the top."

"We look like two gomeys," said Joey.

"Exactly," said Shazer. "Now let's give it a few minutes and we try that bar again."

The lads waited a while and headed back up to the same bar they were refused entry. The bouncer put his hand out to stop them. "Alright lads. Where were ye tonight?"

Shazer answered the bouncer with a laid-back plum accent. "We're just coming from Barry's in Douglas. We said we'd come in for a few sherbets."

The bouncer folded his arms back up to his chest. "Enjoy the night lads."

The lads walked into the bar and saw the place was thronged with women.

"I can't believe that worked," said Joey all excited to be finally left into a bar."

"I know yeah," said Shazer, "and there's women all over the shop, get in the gatts you, I must just go for a piss."

On his way to the toilet, Shazer saw two frumpy looking girls having a chat.

Putting on the same posh accent, he engaged them in conversation. "How are you ladies? You look like you're having a good convo. Do I know your face from the campus?"

"Do you attend MTU?" asked one of the girls.

"Ehh…I finished up last year, but I hate talking about college when I'm out," said Shazer.

"We were just talking about plant-based foods, that can be an alternative to meat," said the other girl.

Shazer looked at the girl with surprise "WOW, are you vegan too?"

The two girls responded with energetic excitement, "Yaaaah."

Just then Joey arrived down with the drinks. "Here Shazer, you should see the state of the fean up there with a purple mohican, how the feck was he get left in before us."

Shazer nudged Joey, then whispered into his ear, "Play

wide will-ya, I'd say we could score with these aul-dolls."

"By the way I'm Seamus and this is my friend here Joseph," said Shazer maintaining his posh accent.

"How's it going," said Joey.

"The girls were just talking about alternative foods that can be used instead of meat...Joseph is vegan too," said Shazer to Joey with a wink.

"Oh yeah," said Joey, "I think its messy what they're doing to the dolphins."

"Do you like dolphins too?" asked one of the girls with excitement.

"They're my most favourite creature on planet earth," said Joey.

"So, what do ye do?" asked the girls.

"We're Application Technicians," said Shazer. "But we hate talking about work when were out."

"How about yourselves?" asked Joey.

"We both just finished our exams on political science and have applied for jobs in the civil service."

"Gosh that's such selfless vocation," said Shazer. "Kudos to you."

"Isn't it just," replied one of the girls. We're also involved in our local constituencies…I'm with Fianna Fail, and she's Fine Gael. How about you guys?"

"WOW we all have so much in common," said Shazer. "But we hate talking about politics when were out."

****

Then next day the boys wake up in the girl's apartment on the Western Road. "Well girls, we're off. We'd love to stay longer but I always pick up the litter in my local area on Saturdays," said Shazer.

"And I must go look at adopting a greyhound this morning," said Joey.

"See-ye-laaater," said the boys waving goodbye.

As they walked out on to the street, the two boys gave each other a hi-five. "That was easy," said Shazer.

"I know yeah," said Joey. "I'm starving after all that… how about we head down to Tony's Bistro for a fry?"

"With extra rashers," said Shazer.

"Now you're talking," said Joey.

Just then the girls shout out their window, "Guys… hey you guys, you forgot your hats."

Shazer looked up at the girls hanging out their window. "Why don't ye hold on to them for keep-sakes, well call ye during the week."

"Okaaaay chat with you soon," shouted the girls.

"Did you get their numbers?" asked Joey.

"Nah," replied Shazer.

"Me neither," said Joey.

The lads leave Tony's Bistro rubbing their belly's "If I eat anymore sausages, I'll turn into the Taoiseach," said Shazer.

"I know yeah," said Joey "Time for a haircut."

"What are you always getting haircuts for?" asked Shazer.

"I like to keep meself well groomed."

"But a haircut every week is a bit overboard," said Shazer

"Look, let you go to the bookies and I'll follow you up when I'm finished me bazzer," said Joey.

After placing a few bets, Shazer got tired of waiting and headed up to the hairdressers to call Joey. On arriving, he saw a woman in her 40s with enormous breasts giving a haircut to Joey, with his head plonked firmly between her massive cleavage.

With a facial expression nothing short of Aphrodite massaging his central nervous system, Shazer interrupted "So that's why you're always getting your haircut?"

Joey annoyed that he was rudely disturbed, started getting ratty, "Shut will-ya, I come in here all the time."

Shazer looked at his phone, "Well hurry on will-ya, I've some missed calls and a text from Francie."

"What does he want?" asked Joey

"He said he couldn't get a cab home last night from West Cork and can we come down to collect him. He said to get a loan of the pick-up off Luke, and to let Finbarr out of the van. He sent on the Eircode."

"Come on so, we see how Francie got on last night," said Joey.

The lads arrived in a small fishing village somewhere down West, and pulled up to the house, beeping the horn.

Francie came out to greet them. "Nice one for coming down boys, I've a small job I must do before we leave."

Breeda waved over at the lads, then said to Francie, "Are you sure it's not too much trouble for you Francis?"

"It's no trouble at all Breeda, I'll be only too happy to help you out."

Breeda opened an agricultural shed packed with copper and other scrap metal.

"It's an awful mess," said Breeda. "My husband was a terrible hoarder."

"Don't you worry about that at all Breeda, I'll have it all gone by today for you."

"Are sure you won't take any money?" asked Breeda.

"Your money no good with me," said Francie.

"Thanks, so much Francis, you're a thorough gent," smiled Breeda.

Francie approached the lads. "Right boys, give me a hand clearing out that shed and there'll be a few quid in it for ye."

"Sounds good to me Francie," said Shazer.

"Me too," said Joey.

The lads loaded up the pick-up with scrap metal and headed off out the drive waving goodbye at an elated Breeda.

"Where to now Francie?" asked Shazer.

"Hammond Lane scrap yard," said Francie.

While driving back the Cork Road, Joey spotted a new age traveller hitchhiking. With thick matted hair tied up in bun and colourful clothes he sticks out his thumb. "Don't forget to pull in for your-man," said Joey with excitement.

"You read me mind," said Shazer. "I'm doing it as we speak."

The boys pull in some distance up the road from the hitchhiker.

Then Joey shouted out the window, "Hurry on willya, we haven't got all day."

In a panic, the hitchhiker scrambled to pick up his bags and run up to the pick-up. Just as he reached the door, the boys speed off with the wheels spinning, and the sound of laughter coming from the cab, screaming "WoooHooooo…see ya later Crusty."

"Ahhahaha for feck's sake, that never gets old," smiled Shazer.

Francie laughed out loud and said to the boys, "Haahaa. Imagine getting caught for that old chestnut."

"Shur, he could do with the exercise. Aren't we doing him a favour?" laughed Joey, bringing much amusement to the three boys as they drove home.

As they drove through Blackpool, Francie spotted two lads with an approximate combined weight of 37 stone sitting on a wall. "Pull in there Shazer for two minutes."

Shazer pulled over the pick-up and Francie got out to talk with the lads. "Alright boys, are ye going for a few scoops tonight?"

"We donno yet," replied the lads.

"Look, how about I get ye a bag of cans for 10 minutes work?" asked Francie.

"What must we do?" asked the lads.

"All ye have to do is lie down on the back of the pickup and then I'll take ye to the off-licence."

"OK so," said the lads.

Francie opened the back of the pick-up, and the lads climbed in before he covered them with bits of sheet metal."

"Right Shazer, off to the scrap yard," says Francie.

"What are ya doing with the two boys in the back?" asked Joey.

"Shur don't they weigh the vehicle before we go in, and the more the weight the more money," said Francie.

The two boys burst out laughing.

"Your one hungry article if I ever met one," laughed Shazer.

The lads drove into the scrap yard, and the pick-up was weighed. Then Shazer drove down to the end of the yard and Francie told the heavy lads to get out and wait for them by the front gate.

On the way out, the vehicle was weighed again when empty, and Francie collected his payment in the office.

"Clutching a wad of cash, he waved the notes saying "Nothing wrong with that-lah.""

"Not too bad at all," said Joey.

While driving out the gate, the two heavy lads wave the pick-up to pull over and collect them.

"What about the boys Francie?" asked Shazer.

"Keep driving," said Francie.

"That's bad form," said Joey.

"Shur, they could do with the exercise. Aren't we doing them a favour?" said Francie with a smirk. The three lads burst out laughing as they drove down the road.

Suddenly Francie remembered with a shout, "Where's Finbarr?"

"Oh, for feck's sake," said Joey. "We left him out for a run at Breeda's house and forgot to take him with us."

"Right boys, drop me off at the van straight away. I'll have to go back down and get him. The poor fellas probably looking for me," said Francie.

Francie drove the van back down to West Cork and arrived at the house only to see Breeda in the porch with Finbarr wrapped up in a blanket.

"Oh Breeda, am I glad to see the two of you. I thought Finbarr was lost."

"He was in a bad way Francis when you left, but I managed to calm him down," replied Breeda.

"I'm after having a long day," said Francie. "Would it be ok if I had a shower?"

"I'll do you one better Francis. How about I'll run you a nice warm bath, and when you come out, I have a chicken ready in the oven?"

"Oh Breeda, that sounds great," said Francie.

As Francie was splashing away enjoying his bath, he heard the voice of a young woman inside the kitchen. "Mammy…mammy I've brought you an apple tart."

Francie got out of the bath to dry himself, when he noticed there's no towel in the bathroom.

He stepped out of the bathroom stark naked calling for Breeda. "Breeda have ya any towel?"

Breeda saw Francie in the bedroom and handed him a towel when suddenly they both jumped to the sound of a terrifying scream.

"Oh MY GOSH…Maaammeee…you didn't!"

Breeda looked and saw her daughter who was almost choking on a piece of chicken. "Now now Fionnuala it's not what you think."

Fionnuala screamed. "What are you doing here in my mammy's bedroom naked, you fecking fucker?"

"For fecks sake," said Francie with his hands on his head. "Not again."

"Cover yourself up immediately," roared Fionnuala. "How dare you expose yourself in front of my mother."

"Its not what you think dear, this is Francis he's a friend of mine, I feel terrible this will your first impression of meeting each other" said a mortified Breeda.

"We've already met mother," snarled Fionnuala. "He tried to rob Máiréad knickers yesterday."

"What! Is this true Francis?" asked Breeda with a stunned look of concern.

Equally stunned that he could ever feel so uncomfortable in such circumstances, Francie muttered under his breath, "*Shur she ran off without her knicker like she was forgetting her lipstick.*"

"What did you just say?" asked Fionnuala full of inquisition.

"That's not what happened at all, at all," replied Francie.

"Well, what happened so, why don't you tell us so Francis," said a sarcastic Fionnuala.

Standing naked between the two women Francie noticed Breeda's eyes were beginning to well up with tears, then channelling his inner social democrat he paused, holding both her hands with a firm yet sincere grip, replying, "Breeda that young lady misplaced her personal effects at a job I was working on, and with the upmost discretion, I felt Máiréad's story belonged her, and wasn't mine to share."

With a teardrop rolling down her cheek Breeda smiled with joy, "Oh Francis, how very noble of you, I knew there must have been logical explanation."

"THAT'S IT. I'm going to call the Guards," cried Fionnuala.

"NO NO NO, there's no need to call the Guards," said a panicky Francie.

Breeda intervened. "Now now Fionnuala, why don't you go outside and get some air, and we'll talk about this in a few minutes."

Fionnuala stormed out of the room.

"Sorry about that Francis," said Breeda. "She's never really got over the loss of her father. I'll speak with her now and try and calm the situation," when all of a sudden, they could hear another terrifying scream coming from the back of the house.

Breeda ran out right away with Francie following behind her with a towel wrapped around his waist.

"What is it, pet?" asked Breeda in a panic.

Fionnuala stood shaking, pointing at the ground, which was scattered with bloody feathers. "What happened to Henry, mammy?"

"Oh, Fionnuala dear, little Finbarr was in an awful way earlier on, and got in to the coup." said Breeda doing her best to console Fionnuala.

"But I've had him years," cried Fionnuala. "He was happy out living his best free-range life."

"Come on inside love, and we'll have a cuppa tea and some apple tart," said Breeda.

"You, ya bastard. It's all your fault," said Fionnuala to Francie, who was now standing in a mess of bloody feathers with only a towel around him.

"I'm going in there to change," said Francie as he tried to kick the plasma-stained plumages off his feet.

"Come on in, dear, and sit down," said Breeda.

While sitting at the kitchen table, Fionnuala cried with her head in her hands mourning the brutal murder of Henry. Looking up, she noticed the chicken on the table. "Where did that chicken come from, mammy?" she asked.

"Don't worry about that at all love," said Breeda.

"No! tell me now…I want to know!"

"Fionnuala love, it would be an awful waste not to harvest an animal."

"NOOOOOOOOOOOOOO!" screamed Fionnuala, "…don't tell me I'm just after eating Henry's little wing?"

Breeda left the kitchen and knocked at the bedroom door. "Sorry about all this Francis, I'm going to have to talk with her, it may take a while."

"No problem at all Breeda…shur seeing a strange man starkers in your mother's bedroom, would be a shock for anyone…take your time," said Francie.

"Would you be a dear and light the fire for me please?"

"I will, of course, go in and do what you have to do," said Francie.

****

Francie sat on a stool in the sitting room and began to light the fire when Breeda and Fionnuala entered the room.

"What do you think you are doing?" snapped Fionnuala as she stared at the black smoke flying up the chimney.

"Your mam asked me to light the fire for her," said Francie.

"Are you burning the recycling?" queried Fionnuala.

"Ah shur they're great for lighting the fire," says Francie.

"ARE YOU FREAKING SERIOUS!" screamed Fionnuala "They were supposed to be recycled. What about all the carbon emissions?"

"Ahh shur you save a fortune on firelighters," said Francie.

"GET OUT…GET OUT OF OUR HOUSE!"

Francie looked at Breeda. "I think its best if I head off there for a while."

"Do Francis. Why don't you go down to the local for a pint, and I call you when we're done." Breeda then lowered her tone speaking under her hand. "She can be very feisty when she wants to be."

Francie replies to Breeda with a wink "Black cat, black kitten."

"Stop it Francis, don't make me laugh," smiled Breeda.

After heading down to the pub in the village, Francie sat at the counter. "I'll have a pint of Murphy's."

Then he heard a strong French accent asking him a question. "Hey Paddee, are you a fisherman?"

Francie turned his head to see who was talking to him. "Who'd ya think you're calling Paddy, Froggy?"

The Frenchman laughed, "Ahhh the Irish humour, I just love it."

"Yeah, well. I'm in no humour, so leave it off," said Francie.

"Don't tell meee, you've got wooman problems…I know know wooman problems when I see it," said the Frenchman.

"I'd say you know a lot about that alright," said Francie.

The Frenchman laughed and said to the barman, "I'll pay for that pint."

"Thanks," said Francie, "I'll get the next one."

"So, what is it Paddee, did she break your heart? You look like you don't have a heart to break," laughed the Frenchman with a growl.

Francie grined, "That used to be the case alright."

"Let me give you some advice Paddee…when fighting with your wooman it just makes the love making more passionate…believe me I knoow."

"Feck it," said Francie "Pepe-le-pew wouldn't tie your shoelaces."

The Frenchman laughed again, "I know how to make the woomans swoon, us French are a romantic people."

"Yeah, I'd say they wimmin go mad for the garlic breath alright," said Francie.

"Nooo, not the garlic, the oysters…I have some back in my boat if you like."

"Have ya any chickens?" asked Francie. "Not chickens Paddee, oysters the food of love."

"Shur they're manky yolks," said Francie.

"I take some oysters back to my wooman, when she is mad, I dance with her in the kitchen, pushing and gyrating to the music."

"We call that a mock-jock in Cork," said Francie

The Frenchman continued, "Then I kiss her neck, caress her body, speak passionate words, carry her to the bedroom and make passionate love to her all night long… and that's how I make the woomans go crazy."

"Sounds like she could do with a defibrillator," said Francie.

"Of course not, Paddee…what do you do to drive the woomans crazy?"

Francie thought about the question, then answered, "Well I suppose I'd head off out for a few pints."

"Yes," said the Frenchman.

"And then I'd stop off at the chipper on the way home."

"Do you get oysters?" asked the Frenchman.

"Nah," said Francie. "I get a fish supper."

"Having greasy chipper all over your face doesn't sound very romantic to me…what do you do next?"

"Well, I'd probably head off up to bed, you know yourself," said Francie with a wink.

"With passionate kissing?"

"A shur, there be no kissing," said Francie.

"All night long?" asked the Frenchman.

"Err..it wouldn't be all night now at all," said Francie.

"What..and that is it?" said the Frenchman shocked. "But what do you do to drive her crazy?"

Francie again takes his time to think, then answered, "Well, I wipes me gob off the pillowcase alright, that drives her crazy all together."

The Frenchman burst out with laughter and slapped Francie on the back. "Very good, Paddee; like I said, I just love the Irish humour."

Francie called another round when he got a phone call from Breeda. "You can call back up Francis, Fionnuala is after calming down a little."

****

Back at Breeda's house, the fire was roaring, and Francie sat down in the front room. "Well, how is she?" asked Francie.

"She was grand until she tried to call her brother from my phone and saw our text messages.""What ones?" asked Francie.

"The one about the two dogs being stuck together." "What one was that?" asked Francie.

"The one where you said they'd have to throw a dish of boiling water on us, for us to separate," said Breeda.

"Oh, I remember now," said Francie. "That actually happened to Finbarr before with a sheepdog."

"He's like his owner so, for the country girls," joked Breeda as she got up to pull the curtains.

As if to have an epiphany, Francie smiled tenderly at Breeda, admiring the iridescent twilight dappled upon her face. Sitting down together by the fireside, he warmly looked into her eyes, resting his hand upon hers, softly expressing, "Breeda, not many people get who I am, and I know you can tell I haven't lived a perfect life, but if this is what the final stretch is going to look like for me, all my imperfections have been worth enduring, just to be sitting here with you."

Breeda smiled back at Francie squeezing his hand, "Shur we can all be misunderstood Francis…we can all be misunderstood."

FIN

Link to the ebook edition of A Misunderstanding in Cork City.

Please Review

Dear reader,

If you enjoyed this story, I would really appreciate if you could spread the word and leave a review on Amazon or Goodreads. Your opinion counts, and it influences buyer decisions on whether to purchase the book or not. Reviews can also open doors to new and bigger audiences for the author and helps get this book into the hands of those who most need to hear its message. Thank you.

Emmett

About the Author

Emmett Corbett is an Irish writer, poet, and lay litigant who has brought constitutional issues before the Supreme Court. Drawing from lived experience, his work confronts the hypocrisy, stonewalling, and absence of accountability within Irish state institutions, while capturing the spirit and struggle of working-class life.

He is also the author of a poetry book called *Poetry Within The State*. This collection shares potent insights of social critique, entwining strands of hypocrisy and double standards with threads of injustice stitching through the fabric of today's society.